Allured, I Await

Vedha L.Krishnan

Allured, I Await
Poetry

by   Vedha L. Krishnan 2023 ©
Book cover design : Keshika Suntharalingam
First Edition : January 2023
Pages: 72
ISBN : 978-93-5533-531-9
Aelay Publish
Contact : +91 9944992571
Designed by : Aelay publish team

Like lightning you came,
Without warning,
Fuelled me up,
To reach you.

Preface

The making of this book started as a way to journalize the thoughts and emotions that struck me to the extent I couldn't sleep unless I verbalised it. Little did I know, that those words would come out as a poetry book.

I publish these poems in the hope that others might also get motivated to find and enjoy the creative outlet that reaches out to their heart.

These poems voice out the making of a true warrior in life, people who inspired me on the way, few questions each of us go through in life, and about the one who made my heart flutter for the first time.

I am eternally grateful to my family, friends, well-wishers and those who were critical in inculcating valuable lessons in me, through ways favourable or unfavourable to me, for every experience has shaped me the way I am now, at a much better place than I was before.

I believe that words have the power to transform the future. I sincerely hope that through these lines, people who feel lost in life, find the necessary ingredients to heal and take a step forward towards their higher purpose of existence.

Contents

Humble abode

Surreal world

The soothing breeze,
Calms down your inner turmoil,
The delicate butterflies,
Entices the buried joy,
Earthy smell,
Leaves you feeling blessed,
The rustling leaves,
Keeps you company.

All of this transports you,
To a different world,
The world it was meant to be.

* ★ *

Awaited getaway

You've got a free pass,
To an unknown place,
Can get carried away,
For you don't need to load luggage,
Or coordinate your stay.

Everything will be taken care of,
For the cost of suspense,
It could be a dreamy world tour,
Or just a home tour,
A wild safari, or a survival challenge.

A cliché vacation,
Where you meet random people,
Acquaint with some, bid adieu to many,
Disputes with a few, get hurt sporadically.

Whether you get a feast,
Or starve sick in survival,
Largely depends,
On the coupons you receive,
Based on how well you coped,
With your former getaway.

You are not going to skip your turn,
Uncertain of the outcome,
Because come what may,
You always enjoy the idea of a vacation,
You easily forget little mishaps, and get forward,
Embrace, whatever exciting experience it offers,
Cause this is not a home away from home,
But a Vacation after all.

Soil body

This fertile piece of earth,
Enriched with all that's needed, for it to grow,
Stays a lump,
Letting in anything coming its way,
Getting drained,
From getting dumb.

Not knowing the plastics from manure,
Takes in a lot, unknowing the toll,
When the dryness kicks in,
Questions the water,
Of not providing enough,
How much depth of parchedness, will it take,
For this soil to know what is to be thrown,
How many seasons should it pass?
Before it chokes.

Making of a warrior

Thank you, but sorry

Thank you, fragile things,
For keeping my heart still unbreakable,
The anger I unleash upon you,
Keeps me from damaging,
My subtle heart.
What would I do if you didn't exist?
As the hope to rise,
Sinks further each time.

Thank you for taking in my sorrow,
For if I show it to fragile minds,
They blame me for being expressive,
Thank you, God, for these fragile things,
Thank you, but sorry.

Candid heart

This longing heart,
Knows no formality,
Welcomes and provides,
When it feels touched.

What difference it would be,
When it can beat for every moment,
In rhythm with life,
Even when untouched, unplanned.

* ★ *

Blessed with anger?

I envied those who showed their anger,
Not minding the hurt they might inflict,
It brings out the best,
As anything suppressed, is only waiting to erupt,
The volcano of dormant anger will melt,
Your hardened heart, if not extinguished with kindness,
But alas! to forget or forgive is unlike humans,
Resentment can keep you away, from hurting others,
The result although, is not promising,
As it destroys your trust in people, their promises, your hopes,
Only with time you realize, that manifesting anger is not a blessing,
What matters, is the time you give yourself, before exploding abrasively.

Don't like me for who I am

The fireflies have lost their gleam,
Parched lands stay deserted,
Who would adore them,
For dullness? For Droughtiness?

Don't like me for who I am,
For I may alter, as time glides,
Like me for what I have lost,
Cherish me for what I might become.

Like me for enduring the pain I felt,
As I let go a part of me, dismayed,
Empathize for the silent scream I voiced,
As I sutured my torn heart, without any aid.

With time and words,
Springs could seep through the cracks,
The 'unexpected' could happen,
Only if, you don't like me,
Just for who I am.

* ★ *

Best of the worst

There comes a speed breaker in your life,
When you, consciously are willing to accept,
A slightly sickening selection,
Choosing the best of the worst,
When it's too much of a load,
On your heavy heart,
To come to terms, with the worst.

This option though,
Comes with a rewarding outcome,
You no longer need the better,
Cause you are ready to settle,
For a Bland normal.

Insanely happy

Alright,
The one I want is here,
For real,
Eternal,
I'm beaming with joy,
Dancing in delight,
I'm full of happiness,
Running or resting doesn't matter,
Grinning wide,
Mad as a hatter.

Insanity is in both ends,
What to do with this unlimited supply,
When I don't know to hold a handful of it?

Should I go announcing,
Or sprinkle a little of it everywhere?
Just the thought, that I'm happy all the time,
Would start to affect me,
I'll have to handle the optimism,
Just as I learn to handle the harm.

Sources of inspiration

A flower, she be

She suffered a lot,
From growing up as a bud,
To gathering the courage to face the world,
Who would have told the flower,
The duties she had to do,
Be it the scorching sun, or a gloomy rain,
She had to bear it all,
All for what?

Collecting the heavy rain dew on her lap,
Blooms up to become a comforting visual,
Balances the unpredictable reality,
All with just a thin stalk,
At all cost,
She mustn't wither, mustn't fade,
Bears it all,
All for what?

Naively sacrifices her essence,
Not minding that people leave her empty
After extracting her fragrance,
I buzz around saying,
"Don't worry dear flower,
For I won't forget the warmth of your petals,
Won't forget the sweet raindrops you captured,
Won't forget your captivating beauty,
For my precious flower you'll always be.
You have always been my strength,
Was always there when I needed you,
Sorry, for not sharing the brutal climate, you faced,
For if I get a chance,
Would take away your blues".

But nature felt it would be unfair,
So, I transformed into an eternal bee,
Who would always stay,
By your side,
To tell you,
You've blossomed into the most beautiful flower,
I've ever seen,
Be happy my dear flower,
For my precious flower you'll ever be.

Unsung hero

Right from when life starts from zero,
He's always there, my unsung hero,
Right there, supporting the warmth,
The warmth I needed the most.

He's a soldier, ready to protect,
His household realm, and my courage,
Might not have won great battles,
But definitely won a place in my heart.

The one passive in engaging, seemingly,
Executing efforts to action, tenaciously,
This hero knows, no stage, no theatre,
Other than the platform called home.

An assuring lap to sleep on journeys,
Secure shoulder to lean,
When troubled,
By enemies, hidden or striking,
He is the unsung hero,
In my life.

Just like that

She comes like the drizzle,
Very gentle to touch,
Enlightening my mood,
Just like that.

She comes like the torrent,
Harsh and hurting,
Makes me regret,
Just like that.

Whether its mild or stormy,
The raindrops come to hide your tears,
She comes to save me,
Just like that.

My butterflies

They came to me,
Without a welcome,
Without any hesitation,
My butterflies.

They wiped away my tears,
Without expecting the same,
Without feeling weary,
My two butterflies.

I might have shut them away,
For reasons, known or unknown,
But, they flew, back to me,
My winged friends.

They brought out the childish joy,
Which I had kept hidden,
For I, being hurt, as an adult,
Wanted to save the spark left.

I might have abandoned them,
And gone into my shell,
But they waited for me,
My beautiful butterflies.

I am grateful to both of you,
For the time you spent,
Will remember you, till the end,
Not in debt, but to depth,
Even after death do us apart,
Because you made me realize,
The world is warm after all.

The perfect break

Is she meditative,
Or under some spell,
I see her from my balcony,
She's sitting at the terrace,
Looking blank into emptiness.

A middle-aged lady,
She stares with no intention,
With undivided attention,
Maybe to divide from her current state.

Few clothes lie beside her,
Scattered with clips,
The remaining task hangs on the strings,
Waiting for her to finish.

What was that thing,
Which made her to sit,
With perfection in her posture,
Surrounded with imperfection.

For her, it seemed perfect,
The perfect time to pause,
From her mundane life,
The perfect way to embrace,
Who she is.

On the way

I came past,
An aged man with a cane,
Just a passer-by, I thought,
Stretched his palm towards me,
Overcome with sympathy,
Fortunate, I felt,
For giving him the price,
That would fetch him, a cup of rice,
How petty,
When I dine thrice.

I came past,
An aged man, with a smile on his face,

The non-deceiving type,
Having high hopes,
On every encounter,
Even when the others, brushed him away,
Unfortunate, I felt,
For leaving the place,
Without knowing the lesson,
That made him that way.

Making of a warrior -2

Lesson on the way

A lesson is on the way,
For every stone you turn,
It's like none other,
Will never disappoint you,
Like the faith you have in others,
Sure to teach you good,
Even if you take it badly,
It's like an alarm, that automates on its own,
To put an end to all the delusion, you've built.

A lesson is on its way,
Unless you live in a magical land,
Where things go as planned,
The way you want it to be,
Or at least never in the way,
Of not keeping you happy,
It's a blessing in disguise,
If it rings at the right time,
Cause even if it's snoozed for now,
You will have to face it,
Eventually,
Maybe, in a more disturbing way.

* ★ *

The most important thing

Ever wondered the reason for your existence?
Never feel happy just by making ends meet,
Cause it's a blessing to be born a human,
Utterly pointless, if you live like a robot.

The machines have commands,
They follow it till their end,
Can never improvise, nor be creative,
Following the duties, almost like us.

We live most of our lives,
In guessing, manipulating,
Out of control, or under custody,
All of us trying to be sane.

The most important thing in life,
Is not just to survive,
By being in control,
But to love and care for the little things,
The Little things,
That could bring joy to others.

* ★ *

Ready...or not?

Looked like I was ready,
From a certain point till now,
Thought I had become steady,
More capable somehow,
Until,
My breath stopped without a forecast,
My framework succumbed,
Before I lost vision to the happening,
Paralyzed,
All I could think of,
Was, I went unnoticed,
Wailed for recognition,
With my benumbed voice.
Proved to be a laughing stock,
Me, towards myself,
An element as simple as a dream,
Had patted the ignorance out of me,
At last.

Word boomerang

A word said,
An emotion lost for one,
A word said,
An emotion hurt for one.

Do the efforts of the past mean nothing,
Or are they lost, along with the words,
Life is to be taken lightly,
Or, should it not be?

A boomerang returns,
From where it was tossed,
A word returns,
From where it was said.

* ★ *

Imperfectionist

Take away my hurdles,
I have faced enough,
Let everything around me freeze,
So, I can move, and embrace the warmth,
Which the striving 'I' deserve.

Just do this one more thing,
I will ask none other,
Yet another deceiving promise I make,
So, you pity me, for the hopeless swindle,
And grant me the never-ending last wish.

If I got, what I truly deserve,
It would be nothing more than a mirage,

If he got even half of my gratefulness,
It would be unfathomable.

He is whom I call,
The Divine Imperfectionist,
For he never complained, or punished,
When I didn't thank him, or worse,
Not even acknowledge him.

Well, if he doesn't give me what I want,
How could he be the one?
Returning a favour the exact way ,
Is what would seem perfect ,
And that is exactly what he is doing.

We came here, to live as humans,
He provided us with tools,
To shape ourselves in the best way.
In that process of sculpting ,
Getting hurt, using the wrong tools,
Who is to be blamed here?
The toolbox? The sculptor?
Or the creator ?

* ★ *

Unfinished

Without a kingdom,
I was rented a castle,
I could go through,
The gate house, or the great hall,
Without restrictions,
Feel like a king or any title of honour,
Based on my adoptions.

Without hosting any event,
Or ruling over anybody,
I had got tired of my rented royal place,
Without painting the wall,
Or enjoying the ball,
I wanted to flee this regal place.

To the beholders,
Who thought I should stay,
Put up with it anyway,
Finish decorating the unadorned throne,
I say,
"When building was more rewarding, than maintaining,
When the efforts I slogged, no longer mattered,
I wish to leave the castle unfinished,
As it is".

* ★ *

The path to unlocking

There is a place,
Invisible and without limits,
Where you stay hidden from others,
Where you stay, to find yourself in you,
It can be dark with colours,
Or dreamy in reality,
Busy wavering memories,
Within a stationary room,
The secret door, you will find,
Which can always grant you a cheerful mood,
And such a door you will find,
Only when you show gratitude.

seeking guidance

Dividing to unite

It is where all began,
The foetus disengages,
From its most secure crib,
To become one with the others.

A child loses its grip,
The warm grip of the caring hand,
And wilfully struggles to walk,
To become one with the others.

A person born,
How much ever happy, one may be,
Must grow up, and leave,
Dividing to unite with another.

In the end,
We separate from our will,
From the known,
To explore the unknown,
To become one with the universe,
One where it all began.

⋆ ★ ⋆

One with many

Do what you can,
There's some you can't understand,
Don't bother lurking there,
When you are far from here.

We follow the herd, with this in mind,
There is something meant for each,
And each is different from another.

Whether you choose one out of many,
Or become one with many,
Is a quality you possess,
And any quality is not far from reach for any,
As long as you are open.

Friendship, affection or passion,
We become fixed with one,
Thinking it's the best,
Later, Missing something,
We realize, one is not enough,
We forgot the basic quality of colours,
Red, blue or yellow,
To get all shades,
We need white,
That quality a few possess,
By which they become one with many.

Words with license

Not all words,
Have ownership rights,
Unlike the two,
'death' and 'bliss',
Both happen only once,
And you have license to use them,
When you are there,
Not 'nearly' there.

Of all the things I could borrow,
This one is not in reach,
I could have a near death experience,
Or feel that I am blissful,
But I am only there,
When I have arrived there.

Paradox

A never- ending suspicion,
Of our insight,
This perfect heart,
Couldn't feel,
Emptier than what it feels now.

What do we lose?
What do we find?
Is all that is found actually lost?
Is all that is lost never been found?

A puzzling loop,
Of unanswered questions,
This perfect human,
Could only be more complex than,
What he is now.

Tick-tock

The end of first quarter,
Feels like the beginning of last,
If the end and beginning,
Merge at the same point,
Why is this unavoidable apprehension,
Of missing out,
Something unknown.

Freedom in captivity

I enthusiastically drifted upstairs,
To the terrace,
Thought it would be engaging,
To watch the scenery,
In a cool breezy weather,
As I began to observe,
In what others would have called,
"a beautiful scene",
I felt captivated,
Not by the beauty,
But in my own thoughts,
What was I supposed to do?
I did not feel the happiness,
That would have occurred,
As it did,
A few years back,
The pigeons cooing and flying around,
Workers busy with the construction,
The garments flying in their own space,
Did they also feel the same way?
With nobody to answer me,
I went back,
To my cave,
Where I would no longer feel the same,
As I get to at least observe,
Others talking,
My mind would no longer be free.

* ★ *

Trapped in time

Mystical time,
Rolls in the blink of an eye,
Mystical time,
Traps you in a blanket of lie.

Few hours of bitterness,
Seems torture and why?
While years of smooth sailing,
Glides without a goodbye.

Congested you feel,
Every reckoning second,
It seems as if time was waiting,
To surprise you,
With this nightmare.

Reminiscing is the only key,
In both worlds of time,
Choose wisely to go for the good,
The other will drag you deeper,
To a never- ending misery.

Precious moments are like stones,
You never know when they come handy,
One random spark of happiness,
Is all it takes,
For the dried, withered self,
To burn with passion.

Awaiting

The usual night passes,
Silent tumbling and tossing,
Flustered,
I await.

The spring has blossomed,
In lands and minds,
Still, missing the unknown fragrance,
I await.

What is it that one yearns,
As the more one gets, there is still something left,
What could be that one thing,
Which would leave you, to race the finish line,
Without hoping for another marathon,
Allured, I await.

Flawless footprints

Off late,
I've been paying too much attention,
On the footprints I tread,
As I move forward in devotion,
Towards a destination,
Where my impressions disappear,
As if walking in water or air.

How do I control the depth of my step,
Or the swiftness in retracting my feet?
If I go back to reconstructing the flaws,
That turned out of unawareness,
Or if I go on meticulously decorating,
The upcoming tracks,
I am sure to end up lagging,
Losing my patience,
Even before losing my strength.

Habits die hard,
In-built thoughts die harder,
To create picture-perfect prints,
I need to prepare a precise time every day,
To focus, to remind myself,
Of the path ahead,
So that with every walk,
Irrespective of those who come along,
I will be taking care of my footprints,
Even when I'm overpowered,
By accustomed emotions.

Somehow it seems,
That it would be easier,
To maintain my pace,
If a guiding light flashes by grace.

Underrated love

Yielding the right way

Echoes remain fascinating,
As they follow the voice,
Without interruptions,
Penetrating,
The air around, and other noises.

They seem lonely,
As they trail behind another,
And the one to follow,
Is bound to look lost.

Behind its unperturbed nature,
Lies the persistence,
As they yield and surrender,
To the almighty air.

The struggle with wind,
Or the sounds,
Would be pointless,
Hence,
It chose to give in,
To the one,
Who would carry it,
To places far away,
To places the voice can never see.

First flutter

It had never happened before,
It can never be undone,
My heart fluttered for the first time,
For something inexplicable,
For someone, out of the ordinary.

There was nothing substantial,
But,
Nothing could ever be more ideal,
It was for some pleasing alarm,
Which was beside me, the whole time.

The alarm which tried to wake me up,
From my ignorance,
From my built-up sorrow,
How could you be there for me?
When I haven't done any worthy penance,
Even if I didn't acknowledge your presence.

This sudden burst of emotions,
Strange feeling of witnessing your being,
When I haven't even seen you,
You, my God,
If this is what they call 'unconditional love',
Then, it's what I have for you,
My dear god.

* ★ *

Petty present

The moments in my life,
Where I feel,
The most helpless,
Are not the times when I'm put to challenges,
But when I receive, support and love,
Through the creator, or his creation.

It occurs as if, I am not ready,
To handle it,
And all I can give back,
As a token of thanks is,
Petty tears,
From my melting heart,
Wrapped in congested pain,
From receiving too much.

I deal with difficult things,
In style, comparatively,
But crestfallen,
When subject to,
Devotion,
From the other side,
While I'm living assuming,
Being devoted,
Is only My cup of tea.

Brazen, I label,
My petty present,
With assuring words,
"These tears are no longer contaminated,
With the one I shed for petty things,
As I once used to,
Vowing, that they will remain pure,
Through days to come".

Year-less yearning

Be with me as one,
Be beside me as two,
But,
Not within as one,
That feels like two.

* ★ *

The place I live in

I have moved to a new place,
Unlike all other places I have been,
The address is not far away,
From where I was.

It's exhilarating one moment,
Exhausting the next,
Intense longing lingering,
Sautéed with self-pity and torment.

I love this the most,
Where everybody is named the same,
No one better than another,
Equality at its best.

Seems like it will take a while,
To adjust to my new place,
Without company and convenience,
But I gladly welcome,
Any person, willing to move,
To this place called devotion.

* ★ *

My dearest one

Enough of this hide and seek,
Am I the one hiding, or,
Have I been seeking you,
Without knowing you.

When did this game start?
I accept my defeat,
Now it is time,
You come,
And find me,
If revealing yourself is impossible,
At least make me you,
So that I no longer seek you.

Mischief unmanaged

Flashback,
There's me,
Mischief I was,
All I ever sought,
Was cheerfulness in me,
Cluelessly.

Flash again,
I am here,
Mischievous you be,
All I ever seek,
Is you, in me,
Cluelessly.

A weed I cherish

There is this constant need,
For me,
To nourish a new sapling,
Called greed,
It grows out of proportion,
To the care I give.

This unwelcomed visitor,
Demands that it be given,
A million lifetimes,
To encounter,
The one it has fallen in love,
In all ways, it could be done.

It says,
"I don't want to lose,
Even a single possibility,
Of missing him, and
I can only be destroyed,
By trying all routes,
Of creeping,
Into his heart".

Oh, mysterious one,
Kindly grant this boon,
To my poor guest,
So that it can be sickled out,
From my garden,
Where I have been trying,
To reconcile with you.

Shiva

Drive again,

Into my heart,

Without chains,

I

    Swing

Back

      And

         Forth,

Let me lose control,

And

    Fall

      Upon you.

· ★ ·

www.ingramcontent.com/pod-product-compliance
Lightning Source LLC
Chambersburg PA
CBHW022010170726
47994CB00023B/2823